DATE DUE

JUN 2 7 2005	
AUG 1 9 2005	
APR 0 5 2006	
AUG 1 2 2006	
APR 1 6 2008	
NOV 1 3 2010	
MAY 0 2 2015	
JUL 2 8 2017	

BRIAN'S
HUNT

ALSO BY GARY PAULSEN

Alida's Song • *The Beet Fields* • *The Boy Who Owned the School* • The Brian Books: *The River, Brian's Winter* and *Brian's Return* • *Canyons* • *The Car* • *Caught by the Sea: My Life on Boats* • *The Cookcamp* • *The Crossing* • *Dogsong* • *Father Water, Mother Woods* • *The Glass Café* • *Guts: The True Stories Behind* Hatchet *and the Brian Books* • *Harris and Me* • *Hatchet* • *The Haymeadow* • *How Angel Peterson Got His Name* • *The Island* • *The Monument* • *My Life in Dog Years* • *Nightjohn* • *The Night the White Deer Died* • *Puppies, Dogs, and Blue Northers* • *The Rifle* • *Sarny: A Life Remembered* • *The Schernoff Discoveries* • *Soldier's Heart* • *The Transall Saga* • *Tucket's Travels* (The Tucket's West series, Books One through Five) • *The Voyage of the* Frog • *The White Fox Chronicles* • *The Winter Room*

Picture books, illustrated by Ruth Wright Paulsen
Canoe Days and *Dogteam*

BRIAN'S HUNT

GARY PAULSEN

WENDY
LAMB
BOOKS

Published by
Wendy Lamb Books
an imprint of
Random House Children's Books
a division of Random House, Inc.
New York

Visit us on the Web! www.randomhouse.com/kids
Educators and librarians, for a variety of teaching tools,
visit us at www.randomhouse.com/teachers

Library of Congress Cataloging-in-Publication Data is available upon request.
ISBN: 0-385-74647-4 (trade)
0-385-90882-2 (lib. bdg.)

The text of this book is set in 12-point Galliard.
Book design by Vikki Sheatsley

Manufactured in the United States of America
December 2003

10 9 8 7 6
BVG

*This book is dedicated,
with enormous
affection and gratitude,
to Wendy Lamb—
my friend, my editor.*

CHAPTER

1

He was in his world again. He was back.

It was high summer coming to fall and Brian was back in the far reaches of wilderness—or as he thought of it now, home. He had his canoe and bow and this time he'd added some dried food, beans and rice and sugar. He also had a small container of tea, which he'd come to enjoy. He had a small cook set, and a can to make little fires in the middle of the canoe; he put leaves on to make smoke to drive the flies and gnats and mosquitoes away. He had some salt and pepper and, almost a treat, matches. He still could not get over how wonderful it was to just be able to make a fire when he wanted one, and he never sat down to a cook fire without smiling and remembering when his life in the wilderness had begun. His first time alone.

He dreamt of it often and at first his dreams sometimes had the qualities of nightmares. He dreamt he was sitting there in the small plane, the only passenger, with the pilot dying and the plane crashing into the lake below. He awakened sometimes with sudden fear, his breath coming fast. The crash itself had been so wild and he had been so out of control that the more he had grown in the years since, the more he had learned and handled difficult situations, the more insane the crash seemed; a wild, careening, ripping ride down through trees to end not in peace but in the water, nearly drowning—in the nightmares it was like dying and then not dying to die again.

But the bad dreams were rare, rarer all the time, and when he had them at all now they were in the nature of fond memories of his first months alone in the bush, or even full-blown humor: the skunk that had moved in with him and kept the bear away; how Brian had eaten too many gut berries, which he'd later found were really called chokecherries (a great name, he thought); a chickadee that had once landed on his knee to take food from his hand.

He had been . . . young then, more than two years ago. He was still young by most standards, just sixteen. But he was more seasoned now and back then he had acted young—no, that wasn't quite it either. New. He had been new then and now he was perhaps not so new.

He paused in his thinking and let the outside world come into his open mind. East edge of a small lake, midday, there would be small fish in the reeds and lily pads, sunfish and bluegills, good eating fish, and he'd have to catch some for his one hot meal a day. Sun high overhead, warm on his back but not hot the way it had been earlier in the week; no, hot but not muggy. The summer was drying out, getting ready for fall. Loon cry off to the left, not distress, not a baby lost to pike or musky; the babies would be big enough now to evade danger on their own, almost ready to fly, and would not have to ride on their mother's backs for safety as they did when they were first hatched out.

He was close in on the lily pads and something moved suddenly in the brush just up the bank, rustling through the thick, green foliage, and though it sounded big and made a lot of noise he knew it was probably a squirrel or even a mouse. They made an inordinate amount of noise as they traveled through the leaves and humus on the ground. And there was no heavy footfall feeling as there would be with a moose or deer or bear, although bear usually were relatively quiet when they moved.

High-pitched *screeeeee* of hawk or eagle hunting and calling to his or her mate; he couldn't always tell yet between the cry of hawk and eagle.

A yip of coyote, not wolf because it was not deep

enough, and not a call, not a howl or a song but more a yip of irritation.

He had heard that yip before when he'd watched a coyote hunting mice by a huge old pine log. The log had holes beneath it from one side to the other and the mice could dance back and forth beneath the log through the holes, while the coyote had to run around the end, or jump over the top, and the mice simply scurried back and forth under it to avoid him. The coyote tried everything, hiding, waiting, digging a hole big enough for himself under the log so *he* could move back and forth, but nothing worked. After over an hour of trying to get at the mice, he finally stood on top of the log looking down one side, then the other, raised his head and looked right at Brian as if he'd known Brian was there the whole time, and gave an irritated, downright angry yip. It was, Brian felt, a kind of swearing.

Up ahead four hundred yards, a moose was feeding in the lily pads, putting its head underwater to pull up the succulent roots, and Brian knew it would be an easy kill if he wanted it. Canoes seemed such a part of nature to the animals in the wild—perhaps they thought canoes were logs—and if a person kept very still it was often possible to glide right up next to an animal near the water. In many states it was illegal to hunt from a canoe for just that reason. Brian had once canoed up next to and touched a fawn standing in the shallows. And with feeding moose it was simpler yet; all you had to do was scoot forward when the moose had its head underwater and coast when its head was up, looking around.

Brian had plenty of arrows: a dozen and a half field points with sixty extra points and a hundred extra shafts and equipment to make more arrows, and two dozen broadhead arrows as well as fifty extra broadhead points with triple-blade heads the military had designed for covert work many years before. These were called MA-3s. Deadly. And if sharpened frequently, they were strong enough to reuse many times if you didn't hit a bone or miss and catch a rock.

Looking at the moose, he salivated, thinking of the red meat and how it would taste roasted over a fire. But then he decided against it. The moose was a small bull, probably only six or seven hundred pounds, and nowhere near the fourteen or fifteen hundred pounds a large bull would weigh, but even so it was a lot of meat to deal with and he couldn't bring himself to waste anything he killed. He had gone hungry so long when he had first come to the bush. . . . Food had been everything and the thought of wasting any of it went against every instinct in his body. Even if he made a smoke fire and dried most of it in strips he would still lose some meat. . . .

Still, he could see the shot. Close to the moose,

close in but far enough away to avoid an attack, the bow already strung. Wait until he ducked under to draw the bow and then as soon as the head came up release the MA-3 just in back of the shoulder, under the shoulder blade, and the broadhead would go straight into the heart. . . .

He shook his head. Rehearsals were all right—he did them all the time, came up with imaginary scenarios and how they would play out even if he didn't act.

Like with Kay-gwa-daush. He thought of her often. She was the daughter of the Cree trapping family he had found that first winter in the bush. He had met up with them at the end of winter and had lived with them for three weeks, until spring arrived, and with it, a plane to take him back to civilization.

Kay-gwa-daush's white name was Susan Small-horn but he seemed to be thinking of her more and more by her Cree name. He thought of her constantly. She was his age, came up to his shoulder and a little more, had smiling almond-shaped brown eyes, a full mouth and straight nose and long, thick, richly black hair, and he had never met her. Her father, David Smallhorn, had shown him her picture, and Brian had missed her because she was away at school.

The attempter. That's what her Cree name meant and her family had given it to her because when she was little she was afraid of nothing, would try anything, which had given her a small scar on her left cheek when she was four years old and tried to fire a high-powered rifle. As Brian sat in the canoe, he thought it was almost like the beauty marks women used to wear on their cheeks. Hmmm, beauty mark. Strange to think of it in that way. Strange to think in that flow, scar from rifle to beauty mark. True, she was pretty and that was nice but he did not really know her, but he thought how she might laugh when he met her and told her how his thoughts were running.

The Smallhorn summer camp was north four or five lakes and some river travel from where he sat, perhaps thirty miles. He wasn't sure which lake they were on, but David had told him it was a lake the shape of an arrowhead with a large island on the north end. The island almost touched the land there and they stayed on the island because there were fewer mosquitoes out on the lake where the breeze could get at the camp. It was their permanent summer camp while they waited to move into their trapping area in the fall.

He was heading toward their camp anyway, working north to see new country. Here all the rivers that ran from lake to lake flowed north and west until they poured into the giant Lake Winnipeg and from there the rivers moved north and east to run into Hudson Bay, way up above the timberline.

He had in mind to go see that country. Just head north. South was cities, people, and he was fast coming to think that people, and what people did with their lives, with their world, were not good, were in most cases ugly and wrong.

That was south. Ugly and wrong. And north was country to see, natural country that man had not yet ruined. So he worked north, not in a hurry, in his world, listening to loons and coyotes and frogs and birds and seeing new and beautiful things—sunlight reflecting on the water, blazing red sunsets, black star-studded skies—each day and night.

Sliding, he thought, the canoe was sliding north. And maybe he'd stop and see his friends and meet Kay-gwa-daush and they could have a laugh talking about how his thoughts ran.

Beauty marks from scars.

Ha.

She would laugh.

CHAPTER

2

He glided along the lily pads in the sun, half looking for fish he might eat, and let his mind float back a couple of months. . . .

He had returned to his world, the wilderness. He had sworn that he wouldn't, once he'd gone back to civilization, even when he found out that once he was sixteen he could actually quit school if he wanted to and had his parents' consent. But he didn't want to do that because he had discovered that there was this incredible thing that happened with studying: you learned things.

It sounded dumb when he thought of it, kind of like duh, really, no kidding. But before the plane crash so much of his schooling had been simply getting by, trying to learn just enough to pass the tests and never really *knowing* anything.

When he'd gone back, he started to run into things in books. That was how it had happened at first. He'd been in the bush and survived with only a hatchet because he'd begun to try to learn about things that happened to him; basic things, even idiotic things. You eat the gut berries, you throw up. Don't eat the gut berries.

It sounded silly when he thought of it in that simple way. But when he'd gone back and after the furor over his survival was finished and all the television and media hype was done and all the doctors had examined him to make sure he was "all right," he'd tried to get his life back to normal. But he never really had of course because he had been in a place so completely different. He found that he looked at everything the way he had in the bush when his decisions were a matter of life or death.

If a teacher handed him a history book he didn't just scan it and learn the dates of the Battle of Gettysburg or when Alexander Graham Bell invented the telephone. He had a great thirst to understand, to know things as he'd known them in the bush, to *know*. And so he tried to find out more about everything that came to him, tried to learn about what happened in Gettysburg and came to find that it was not just something in history to take a test about; it was an appalling battle where over fifty thousand American soldiers were slaughtered in three days of horrendous fighting and so thick were the bullets flying at each other that you could *still* find bullets swaged together, because they hit each other in flight and fell to the ground; he learned about the Minnesota First Volunteers, that of 262 who started the battle only 47 were left standing at the end, and most of those were wounded. And Alexander Graham Bell didn't just invent the phone, he was actually trying to find a way to help deaf children communicate with their parents and he came very close to inventing the airplane before Wilbur and Orville Wright.

Brian learned these things. He *knew*.

And though he had come back to the bush now because he couldn't be with the people back in civilization, and because he knew he would probably never fit in, he did not hate school, or the concept of studying and learning.

And he did not hate his parents. He loved them. He'd wanted to see if there was some way he could make the two worlds work together, but he could not; their world was ugly to him and was filled with awful tastes and smells and people who all wanted what he thought were the wrong things; wanted just that, *things,* and money, and the right cars and the right girls and the right clothes. At first he could somehow tolerate how they lived, and he tried to find a way to make it work for him as well. But at the end of two years, he simply could not stand it; he had reached some saturation point, where he could not watch television, could not listen to discordant loud music, could not stand traffic noise, hated the fact that it was never dark at night and he couldn't see the stars because of city light. He went into a state of overload and a kind of shock and open disbelief that people could actually live, or pretend to live, the way they did.

So he had worked out a way to homeschool on his own up here. He had brought some paperback textbooks with him, one on history, another on math, one on nature and biology (he'd already found some errors in that one, especially concerning how animals think or even if they do, clinically, think), several books of literature and of course his Shakespeare, and he'd promised his parents and the school that after he studied them he would take a test to prove he knew these things and then, the next year, they might try more books and more tests.

This procedure wasn't openly accepted, but the school authorities gave him credit for his surviving fifty-four days with nothing but a hatchet—they acknowledged that it showed an ability to learn. Everyone was trying to be flexible because it was clear that he really did want to learn.

There. He stopped, back-paddled the canoe until it didn't move. Under a lily pad, lying still like a small green log, was a large northern pike. Four, maybe five pounds. In some dumb fishing magazine he'd seen in a doctor's office, he'd read an article that said northern pike were not good to eat because they had a series of floating Y-bones down their sides that made it so you couldn't filet them, couldn't cut steaks off the side of them very easily. It also said that they were "kind of slimy." The truth is all fish are slimy because they're covered with an antibacterial coating to keep disease out. The way Brian cooked them, with the guts out but otherwise whole on a flat piece of wood facing a fire, the slime turned a nice blue and came off with the skin. In a cookbook, he found that the French have a recipe called pike *à bleu,* where they bake the fish and serve it on a platter blue from the slime.

Still, he thought, it's a long way from looking at a northern under a lily pad to actually eating one. They were a first-class predator, would take not just other fish but frogs, ducklings and baby loons and now and then had been known to bite people. Like all good predators, they were very fast and very cautious— predators could not afford to be hurt; even a minor injury was a death sentence, because then they could not catch their prey.

He had brought some line and a few small hooks but he rarely used them. It was much easier and more selective to shoot fish with the bow and he'd even brought a few triple-pointed barbed fish heads glued onto the ends of shafts without feathers, just for small fish at very short range. But this was slightly different. The northern was too big for the little fish points, because of the spread of the three points. They wouldn't go into the big fish very far and would just wound it, and the arrow would fall out when the fish thrashed around and it would get away.

He'd have to get a solid arrow with a field point into the head of the fish to kill it and he was lined up all wrong for the kill. He was skirting the lake heading north with the lily pads on the right of the canoe and since he shot right-handed it was awkward to pick up the bow and swing to the right and get a shot off without exposing his whole body, which would probably scare the fish away. The same problem existed if he raised himself in the canoe and tried to turn around and face the other way to get a shot; he had the cargo bundle in front of him with all his gear and he was sitting in the rear of the canoe. If he tried to rise and turn he would undoubtedly scare the fish away. And besides, with the way he was kneeling and with the small amount of room it would be almost impossible to turn.

Still, it was early in the day and there was plenty of light left, plenty of time before he stopped for the night. He crouched down toward the front of the canoe and with careful, extremely slow motions of the paddle he took almost ten minutes, ten crawling minutes to turn the canoe around so it was facing the other way.

Just like so much of what he did now, so much of how he hunted, it was a stalking procedure. He had learned long ago that to hurry is to lose. Patience was the key, the absolutely most important part of hunting anything, from fish to moose. You needed to take the time required. When he was learning more about the north country, he'd read that Inuits hunting seal on the ice would squat over a seal breathing hole for hours, even days, waiting for the seal to come up in the hole to get air. The Inuit would put a small piece of feather over the hole and stand with bone harpoon ready and when the seal came into the hole the air pushing ahead of its body would ruffle the feather and the hunter would lunge with the harpoon and bury the barbed head in the back of the seal. The seal might weigh four hundred pounds and the harpoon didn't kill it but was merely attached to a line the Inuit was holding, so the whole process was very dramatic, like trying to hold a good-sized bull with a piece of string. The hunter had to hold the seal with one hand and probe with another killing spear to kill the seal while it was trying to pull the hunter down through the ice into the water. Needless to say it didn't always work and he read that the hunters were so patient that if the seal never came or they lost it after the first strike they would not be frustrated but merely shrug and go to the next hole. And, Brian learned, polar bears hunted seals the same way, the bear waiting by the hole for a seal to come take a breath—squinting so its eyes wouldn't give it away and covering its black nose with a white paw for the same reason—and when the seal came, the bear lunged down, grabbing it by the nose and pulling the entire three- or four-hundred-pound seal up through a six-inch hole in the ice, pulverizing it, turning the insides of the seal to a kind of stew.

It took that kind of patience. Brian crouched, peeking over the edge of the canoe at the northern all the while, barely moving the paddle until the canoe had completely swapped ends, looking from beneath the water, he hoped, like a slowly drifting and turning log.

It must have worked. Once the fish seemed about to move—its back arched and its gills flared—but a smaller northern came by and Brian could see it was merely defending its territory.

At last the canoe was positioned right and the northern was still there, in a slightly better place because the lily pad was partially covering the fish's eyes.

The bow was strung and, still crouched forward, Brian gently slid a wooden arrow out of his quiver and laid it across the bow, nocked it onto the string, put his left hand on the handle and raised the bow even with the gunwale of the canoe, then a little higher, so the arrow would just clear the side of the canoe.

Then, holding the bow almost sideways, he pushed it while pulling the arrow back, tucked the feathers under his chin, aimed at the bottom edge of the fish to allow for refraction. He'd learned that the hard way, by missing the fish when he'd first started hunting after the plane crash. He released the arrow.

The arrow was slowed only a tiny amount as it traveled through the water and hit the northern with full force just above the right eye. Whether by luck or design it was an almost perfect shot and the shaft slammed through the brain, cutting the spinal cord, stopping halfway through the northern.

The fish, dead in an instant, gave a spasmodic death jerk, a sideways arching of its body, which flung it off into shallower water, perhaps five feet deep. It became still and began to sink, the buoyancy of the wooden shaft slowing the process.

"Ahh," Brian said aloud, "I thought it might float. . . ." All fish have air bladders, which they use to control their depth, and sometimes when they are killed they have enough air in the bladder to make them rise to the surface. Sometimes, as with this northern, the air is expelled and they sink.

Brian was wearing only shorts and he put one hand on each side of the canoe and lift-jumped himself over the side into the water. He slipped beneath the surface with his eyes open and though his vision was blurred and the northern's color made it almost impossible to see, the arrow shaft was a bright white line. He grabbed it and pulled the fish up to the canoe and flopped it over into the boat.

Thank you, he thought, as he always thought when he killed. And then, Good meal, full meal. What he had come to think of as a can't-walk-meal, or a lie-down-and-sleep-meal.

He could not save fish in the summer. If he had a smokehouse or a way to dry the meat without flies getting to it he might be able to keep some, but in the late-summer heat with no refrigeration it was impossible to keep meat for very long and if he tried and ate spoiled fish, it could easily kill him.

He had found a government book on the Internet that had been put out for farmers and hunters and trappers back in the 1930s. It cataloged and described each kind of meat and how to raise the different animals and how to slaughter them and preserve them. There were many surprises, such as the fact that venison, and especially moose meat, were very low in nutritional value and protein while rabbit was the highest. He learned that fish meat was vulnerable to a kind of ptomaine and worse, botulism, which was often fatal. There were documented cases of Native Americans dying from eating dried salmon and other fish because of these poisons. There were also many cases of predators, scavenger birds like eagles, and wolves and foxes and coyotes being found dead from eating bad fish that had died and drifted up onshore.

So he would eat the whole fish, and he smiled remembering the first time: First Fish, and how small it had been and how wonderful it had tasted.

He still felt the same way about it. He still felt wonder at the food, and he looked for a clearing on the bank to make a fire.

Good meal. Full meal. Thank you.

CHAPTER

3

He had changed. He thought at first that he had changed again, that there were steps in how he had done so, but he realized that he was changing constantly as the world around him shifted, as he learned more.

His approach to "camping" was a good example. When he had first been in the bush just after the crash, he had needed shelter and a settled place to be. Or he'd thought he did—he had since decided he'd been wrong to stay with the plane. With his knowledge now he would make weapons and start to move south, hunting as he moved, hunt-traveling.

But back then he had needed a camp and had thought they would find him soon. They hadn't, because he'd been so far off course. And then too he had not had an easy time making fire. To move constantly and try to make a new fire each night with the hatchet and a rock, or at least each time he wanted to cook meat, would have been very slow. Next to impossible.

But he had changed. Now he did not spend an inordinate amount of time on campsites. So he found a clearing in a short time, beached the canoe, made a fire with one waxed match, gutted the fish and threw the guts in the lake, where they immediately attracted small panfish that cleaned them up in moments, and set the northern on a flat piece of wood to cook one side.

It was done in ten minutes and he stripped the meat off the side, still steaming, into an aluminum pot from his cook set and turned the fish over to cook the other side while he ate the first. He had salt but was favoring it less and less. He ate the meat with his fingers, picking carefully through the bones— including the notorious Y-bones—until nothing was left *but* bones and by that time the second half was done. He ate the meat from that, then broke the head open and ate the brain and eyes (he had long ago stopped being picky or squeamish), put the bones and carcass back in the lake where the panfish could get at it and set to his gear.

He was meticulous about his gear and he tried to check everything once a day, starting with the canoe, which was Kevlar and almost bulletproof. Next, the two composite paddles. Then his weapons. He had the bow, a laminate straight, almost a longbow, that pulled forty-five pounds at twenty-six inches' draw. He had tried stronger bows, tested them for a time, and looked at compounds. But they had pulleys and cables and tuning requirements, too tricky to be much good for hard use in the bush.

He checked the bow, and string, and his two spare strings, and then each arrow, using his small stone to touch up the sharpness of the broadheads, which he kept like razors (they could shave the hair off his arms), making sure the arrow he had used on the northern was set to dry right and the feathers would stay straight.

Then his knife. He had a straight-edge hunting knife always on his belt—almost a copy of Second World War Marine Corps–issue knives called K-Bars—and he used the same small stone he used on his broadheads to touch up the blade.

Then a small double-edged cruiser axe that he used as a general tool for cutting wood or setting up a lean-to with the canoe. And then each piece of clothing, checking the stitches and using a sewing repair kit to fix any problems. Next, his moccasins, of which he had three pair, including a knee-high pair that he could fashion into mukluks for cold weather.

He had a light jacket, and a pullover anorak that came down to his knees made of breathable waterproof cloth and two Polarfleece pullovers to wear under the parka and two pair of Polarfleece pants and four pair of brown jersey gloves, which he found to be as good as anything. He could not stand a hard winter but he was good for anything less—way better than he'd been for his first winter—and when all the gear was checked he boiled some water from the lake and made a pot of tea and when it had cooled he drank the whole pot and leaned back against a log nearby and sat watching the fire, his stomach full, evening on its way and a drowsy mood coming over him.

He had a sleeping bag in the canoe, a good five-pounder that would keep him warm to ten above, and a closed-cell foam pad for a mattress. He thought of getting them out and setting up a land camp to spend the night but decided against it.

The bag was really too much for weather this warm. If there wasn't strong wind and it didn't rain, he had taken to sleeping in the canoe out on the lake. He had a small grapnel hook with dulled, rounded points, only four inches across, and a hundred feet of light nylon line, and he would drop the hook and let it bite into the weeds and mud on the bottom and feed out enough line to hold the hook down and in place and then tie it off to the bow of the canoe and unfurl his pad in the bow, in front of the cargo, and sleep there with the cargo and its covering tarp for a pillow.

Most of the lakes in the north country were shallow, scooped out by ancient glaciers, rarely over fifteen or twenty feet deep, and if the wind didn't come up it was like sleeping in a cradle. Usually, out on the water a way, the mosquitoes were not much of a bother. It was late summer now and they were not as bad as they are in the first part of the year, when driven by the need to hunt and get blood and lay eggs before fall. In the first hatch in summer Brian had seen swarms so bad they plugged his nostrils—lord, how he'd hated them when he'd first crawled ashore from the plane crash. They had torn him apart.

Dark was coming now and he made sure the fire was out, loaded his gear back in the canoe and paddled out offshore a hundred yards. Here he stopped the canoe and drifted for a few minutes, checking the weather. But the sunset was beautifully calm, serene, and not a breath of wind, and he nodded and slid the hook over the side until it hit the bottom, then back-paddled until it bit, tied it off to his bowline and arranged his bed to sleep on top of his bag because the air was still warm and mellow. He lay down to rest, listening to the evening cry of loons calling to each other across the mirrored water.

A perfect day among many perfect days and the last thought he had before slipping into sleep was that he was in exactly the right spot at exactly the right time in his life.

Perfect.

CHAPTER

4

A strange sound awakened him.

He had been sleeping hard, dreaming, of all things, about Kay-gwa-daush and beauty marks, and at first his body did not want to come up into consciousness.

But so much of him was tuned now to reacting to odd things, a line that did not belong where it was, a sound that should not be there, an odd color or smell. He had almost gone crazy on his last visit back to civilization. Sirens and stink of smoke and bangs and rattles and noise—it had all meshed together and desensitized him to the point where he'd heard nothing because it was so overwhelming.

Here, now, every odd sound or color or line or smell meant something. He had watched wolves hunting once and they would trot or walk along and stop every few feet and look and smell and listen and they checked everything out. *Everything.* Any little rustle in the grass, any soft whisper of sound, every scent.

And now here he lay, awake, knowing only that a strange noise had cut him out of sleep but not what sound or where it had come from and he opened his mouth to clear his ears and held his breath and waited, listening.

The night was perfectly still. The temperature had dropped so that he had without awakening pulled his unzipped bag over the top of him to stay warm, and it was cool enough that even the odd mosquito had gone down and it was so quiet he heard his heart beating in his ears.

But no other sound.

The moon was half full and seemed close enough to touch and made it so bright the lake around him could be seen easily. The canoe rode softly on the slick water, the little anchor still holding well. Nothing wrong there.

He sat up a bit. Nothing on the shore that he could see; of course it was far enough away—a good hundred yards—that even with the bright moon he might not see something small.

But no, nothing. No sound, not even bugs, not even a loon.

And yet he was awake. Why? He trusted his

instincts implicitly here in the bush and he knew there had to have been something, some big or little thing. The dream was not enough to wake him. There had to be some outside influence involved. But he could hear or see nothing. . . .

Wait. There.

A sound. What was it? Very soft, so that he could just barely hear it, and there again, soft, whimpering. . . .

A whine. A soft whimpering whine the way a dog might sound if it was begging or injured.

A dog?

Now he sat and scoured the bank but could see nothing. A coyote, perhaps, brush wolf as they called them up north, or maybe a timber wolf, two wolves, one begging from the other.

He had a small monocular in his pack. Binoculars were too heavy but there were times when he wanted to see things from a distance without disturbing them—he was especially interested in the eagle nests on many of the lakes because he wanted to see the young but didn't want to get too close to them.

He took out the monocular and studied the lakeshore. It was only eight power, but it pulled in a lot of extra light from the moon and he broke the shoreline down into sections and tried to see the wolf or coyote. Or maybe it was a fox.

But there couldn't be a dog out here, could there?

He saw nothing on the first sweep. He looked at the moon and was thinking it was probably two or three in the morning and perhaps he should just accept that it was a coyote or wolf or maybe even a small bear and get some more sleep when he heard it again.

Not louder, but somehow more persistent, perhaps a little longer in duration.

He started another sweep and was halfway through his swing, carefully studying the shoreline foot by foot, when he came to the area where he had made a fire and cooked the northern. And then he saw it.

By the log where he had lain back after eating there was a shape. Not moving, just sitting or hulking, not a coyote but certainly not as big as a wolf either.

A dark shape that might be a small bear—there were many bears in the bush, blacks, some of them cinnamon-colored blacks, and worthy of much respect. He had had a couple of run-ins, one with a bear that he had come close to shooting, another with a bear that had tried to move into his winter shelter and had been driven off by a skunk. But this didn't look quite like a bear either.

Now it moved, stood slowly, and he saw that it had four legs, was slightly larger than a coyote, had a shiny patch on its shoulder, and unless he was completely insane was almost assuredly a dog.

Out here.

And looking at Brian across the water whining, whimpering.

Well, he thought. Just that. Well.

I might as well go see what it wants.

He sat up, completely awake now, and fetched the anchor line from the bow rope and pulled the little grapnel up and paddled toward shore.

Close on he stopped, forty feet from the bank, sixty from the dog, and studied it again. Rabies was a very real disease and while it usually killed the infected animals before they could go far or do much damage, he didn't want to get torn up or killed if the dog was rabid.

He used the monocular again, even this close, because it gathered so much light, and scrutinized the animal. When he had paddled in the dog had come closer to the shore to meet him, but it moved poorly and seemed to favor its right side. Brian held the scope on it to see what was wrong.

It was most certainly a dog—he could see it was a female even in the dark—a nondescript kind of dark-haired malamute cross that the Crees sometimes had in their camps to pull sleds in the winter or pack in the summer. They were not so much sled dogs as just camp dogs and companions that pulled sleds when necessary. And this one seemed friendly enough, wanting to greet him. The dog had that shiny place on her shoulder but otherwise its coat was a dark brown.

And then she turned and Brian saw the shiny spot better and realized that the dog had been wounded in some way, perhaps in a fight, and there was a slash that started just at the top of her right shoulder and went down and back at an angle almost to her rear end. It had bled all down her side, and much of the blood had clotted, but in the moonlight Brian could see the shine of fresh blood.

"Oh man," Brian said aloud, his voice almost startling him because he so rarely spoke, "what in god's name happened to you?"

And the dog whimpered to him again in a sound that it seemed dogs reserved just for talking to humans, a soft asking sound, a soul sound, and Brian dug the paddle in and slipped up onshore to help.

CHAPTER
5

When the dog saw the canoe move toward shore she at first moved to meet it, head down, tail wagging, but Brian hesitated just once more before touching the bank with the bow of the canoe.

This was all very strange, and strange things in the bush often deserved more study. The dog was here, she greeted Brian as a friend, but why? Why a dog? Why was it here? Was there more to it, more people here, something possibly not good waiting for him on the bank?

But he waited just a few seconds because when he was this close the dog first sat, whimpering with pain, and then lay down on her good side with the wound up and waited, just waited for Brian.

It was enough and he pushed up on the bank and jumped out of the canoe. He went to the dog and knelt next to her.

Of course it was still dark but there was the half-moon and he saw that most of the wound, a foot-and-a-half-long rip down the side, was very superficial, just breaking and peeling back the skin, and it had clotted well. Here and there wet blood oozed but even as he watched, it seemed to diminish.

Still, it needed tending to and to do that he needed light, a fire.

"You stay here," he told the dog. "I have to get wood and make a fire."

Either because she understood or perhaps just that she was in pain, the dog stayed by the front of the canoe while Brian moved in the moonlight and found dead wood and dry grass and started a small fire nearby.

He took a burning stick and held it closer to see better and it frightened the dog. "Easy, easy, I have to see it. . . ."

He put his hand on the dog's head and she settled immediately, responding to the soothing sound of his voice. Brian held the light up again and in the relative brightness saw that the rip, however it had been caused, had torn back a flap of shoulder skin about half as big as his palm.

He could see exposed flesh, muscle. Although the meat was not too damaged he knew he would have to fix it in some way, cover it.

"Or sew it up," he said aloud. "I have some fishing line and a needle. I wonder if you would let me sew the flap down?"

He went to the canoe and got out his sewing repair kit. He had thread there but thought it might be too light for the job, would pull out. The fishing line would work better except that he would have to use the large needle with it.

This, he thought, moving back to the dog, could go wrong in so many ways. She wasn't a really large dog—perhaps forty pounds—but she had teeth and Brian had seen dogs fight in the city and had seen wolves kill deer and knew what those teeth could do. He'd read somewhere that the teeth at the back, the molars, even in a moderate dog could come down with twenty-six hundred pounds per square inch. The cross section of the bone in my arm, he thought, is about a square inch. Hmmmm.

Still, he couldn't leave the wound that way.

"I have to hurt you," he said to the dog, petting her head. "I'm sorry, but we have to sew that up. I'll talk and tell you what I'm doing but if we don't sew it and cover it the flies will plant eggs in it. . . ."

All the time he was talking he was preparing himself, kneeling by the dog, threading the fish line through the needle in the firelight—in itself no mean feat—and hoping his talk would soothe the dog.

"I'm going to clean the wound with a little water," he said, dipping water from the lake. He knew it wasn't hygienic but the wound was full of dirt and grass and the water was cleaner than that. He thought of boiling it but then he would have to wait for it to cool and that would take too long. The dog was steady now but might not hold for a long time.

He washed the wound with water as best he could, splashing it gently until the water ran clear without blood or dirt and then folded the flap of skin back up over the wound opening and was dismayed to find that it was too small to cover the space.

It lacked a quarter inch all around, seemed to have shrunk. He would have to pull it and stretch it back while he sewed.

He winced, thinking how it would feel to do it to himself—first stretch his skin and then pull a large needle with fish line through it, again, and again. The dog had remained quiet while he washed and pulled the flap back over—quieter than Brian would have believed—but he did not believe she would lie still for what was coming.

"It's more of a problem than I thought," Brian said. "Maybe going to hurt a little more . . ." Later, much later, he would remember talking to the dog that first night as if she were a person and would not think it odd, never thought it odd. He talked to all animals, deer, birds, wolves, sometimes even fish. But only the dog seemed to understand, seemed to know what he meant.

Well, he thought, here goes, and he pulled the flap, had to tug it sharply into place and took the first stitch with the needle, surprised at how hard he had to push to get the needle through the skin. It was almost like cured leather and he had to exert way more force than he thought the dog would tolerate, just for the first edge. Then he had to pull and tug the flap of skin into position and push the needle through the second edge, again, having to push very hard to get even the sharp needle through the hide, then pull the two edges together with the string and tie a first knot to hold it, then move a quarter inch—which seemed about right—and push-pull it through again. . . .

And again.

And again.

And talking all the while, waiting for the dog to come around and hit him.

"You're such a tough dog. *I* couldn't take this, I know. You must have good genes, tough genes, a tough mother and a tough father, to take this pulling and pushing and poking and just keep taking it and taking it. . . ." His voice even and smooth, trying to calm the dog, ease her mind.

And not once did the head come around. Only at first, when Brian jerked the string to pull the two edges together, was there a reaction, a low, deep rumble from the dog's chest and the head coming up, but it was not a growl so much as a moan and the head never came around, the teeth never bared. The dog just looked at him, looked right in Brian's eyes in the firelight, a look of understanding, of complete and utter trust, and then the head went back down and there were no more rumbles, no more moans, no more glances. She lay there with her eyes closed, content to let Brian work. Almost relaxed.

Thirty-two stitches Brian sewed, each one knotted in place, twenty across the top and twelve down the front side, all about a quarter inch apart, all tightly sewn and pulling the flaps together, and then it was done.

He had a small first-aid kit in the canoe and he took out the disinfectant bottle. It was not enough to have washed the wound but he trickled it in a line along the sewn-up seam edges and it must not have been painless as the bottle said because the dog rumbled again, though she didn't open her eyes or change her breathing.

Then it was done.

Brian cleaned the needle and put the kit away in the canoe, washed the blood from his hands in the lake, found more wood for the fire and built the flames up.

The dog stayed where she was, four or five feet from the fire, and rested. Soon Brian could hear the sound of her snoring over the crackle of flames.

Brian squatted by the fire and let his mind float free, glad the dog was so friendly, glad he hadn't been bitten.

He looked to the east and thought he could see

a glow. Maybe a couple of hours to daylight and then . . . what?

Try to figure it out, he thought. The dog was clearly not wild, clearly friendly to people, had heard-smelled-felt that Brian was out in the lake sleeping in his canoe, had awakened him by whining.

Clearly wanted help.

But where had she come from? There was no collar on her, Brian had checked that right away, and it was a her, not a him, Brian had also seen that, but she wasn't just a loose, wild dog.

She must have come from a trapper's camp somewhere, maybe a Cree camp, perhaps near, perhaps far. She must belong to somebody. But Brian had seen or heard absolutely no sign at all of any people anywhere within miles, and if there had been a camp or people he would know. Animals in the bush react to people, "feel" differently if there is anyone about, and he had not "felt" that difference. Nor had he seen tracks, smudges in the grass, had not smelled smoke.

Nobody was close.

And yet, here was the dog. Obviously a person dog, a dog that wanted to be with humans, a dog that couldn't hunt for herself well—she looked thin—and needed to be with people yet had, for some reason, left her people?

No sense there, Brian thought. He put more wood on the fire and studied the dog in the brighter light.

The dog slept soundly, snoring gently, the wounded side moving up and down. Brian liked the sound of her breathing and he thought of never having had a dog. There had always been some reason his parents wouldn't let him have one. They were too dirty. They shed hair. His mother had allergies. He wasn't responsible enough to take care of a puppy. Lord. Back there. His parents. He shook his head— had that ever been real, that life? That whole silliness?

He watched the wound move with the dog's breathing.

The wound came from a fight with someone or something. It was a slash wound, not from a fall or hitting a stick.

How had it happened?

A fight with another dog? He had considered that possibility while working on the dog. It had been in a major battle with another dog and had been driven out—but Brian wasn't sure if that sort of thing happened outside Jack London novels and he had come to realize that much of what Jack London wrote about the bush was utter nonsense. He might have been a tough man, and he might be a good writer, but he'd also been a hammer-drunk and there was a lot of silliness in what he said about wilderness.

Besides, most people wouldn't let a fight get that far out of hand. A dog that was ripped up that badly couldn't do much work for a while and trapper dogs were used for work, packing, pulling toboggans. And he didn't think a dog that liked people as much as this one seemed to would leave just because of a fight.

So something else.

But nothing else made sense. The dog wouldn't leave her home unless she was driven out and the wound was serious enough. . . .

Wolves? Brian's thinking rolled free. Perhaps the dog was out away from camp, hunting or something, and ran into a pack of wolves. Say they hit her, wound her and in panic she doesn't run home, back to her camp, but runs off, maybe confused, bewildered until she comes to the lake and finds Brian sleeping in his canoe. . . .

No. If wolves had hit her—and David Smallhorn had told him that sometimes they killed small dogs and ate them—she would either have run back into camp or the wolves would have finished her, eaten her. No dog in the world could outrun or outfight a wolf pack.

The wound didn't seem to have been man-made but that was a possible explanation and one that made sense. If a man was cruel enough to injure a dog this badly the dog might run off and not come back, and Brian knew there were men that bad, had read about them, seen them in the news. Beasts. Beast-men.

But the wound didn't seem to be a cut either, did

not seem to have been made by a weapon but by teeth, or claws.

There were some big cats. Brian had seen lynx on several occasions and a forty-pound lynx certainly could inflict a wound like this. But lynx could easily get away from a dog if the dog was foolish enough to chase them, and there were rare mountain lions here in the bush, called panthers or painters in the north country, but the same rule applied. While they could easily wound or kill a dog this way, they much preferred to avoid conflict. They would kill and eat a person rather than tangle with a dog, unless it was very small. Brian had seen several accounts of mountain lions stealing poodles and other small dogs from homes around Los Angeles. One mountain lion there had actually taken a woman who was jogging near L.A., killed her, dragged the body off and eaten part of it.

But not dogs, and that wouldn't explain the dog leaving its main camp.

Deer, moose, could inflict such a wound with their hooves or antlers if attacked, and dogs were sometimes badly injured while trying to attack deer, although more often it was the deer that were injured. Many deer each year were mauled and killed by domestic dogs; people just had no idea how vicious their pet German shepherd could be if it packed with three or four other dogs and ran up on a deer. Or sheep. Or, sometimes, a child.

But again, that wouldn't explain why the dog ran off. Even if she tried to attack a deer and the deer injured her this badly, she would go home for help. Not run off.

And that left what?

Just one animal left in the north woods could do this.

Bear.

One blow with a clawed paw could easily rip a dog in just this manner. And heaven knew they were strong enough to do it. Brian had seen a bear throw a quarter-ton log through the air, looking for grub worms.

But again, it made no sense. If the dog was injured by a bear it would run home, not away.

No sense.

It was almost light. He put a pot of hot water on the fire to boil and make tea. Today would be busy. Like it or not, and he was coming to like it, he now had a family, someone to look after.

The dog would need food and more care and that meant he had to hunt, to kill.

He could take more fish, even panfish to feed the dog at first if he needed to, but in the end the dog would need good meat, red meat, just as wolves needed it.

A moose would be too much but a small buck deer would fill the bill and between him and the dog there would be no waste.

He would first cast for a trail and see if he could pick up sign where the dog had come from, at least a direction, and at the same time see if he could get a deer.

He could think more that evening on how the dog had come to him. Now there was other work.

CHAPTER

6

When he took his bow and quiver in the dawn light the dog tried to follow him.

"No, you have to stay," Brian tried to tell her. Then held out his hand and said more firmly, "Stay!"

But the dog had gotten to her feet, and, still favoring her wounded side, had tried to follow Brian out of camp.

Finally Brian took the anchor line and fashioned a nonslip collar and a leash and tied the dog to the front of the canoe.

The dog could easily chew through the cord and follow him anyway but she finally seemed to understand with the line tied that she was supposed to stay. At first she sat and watched while Brian walked away, and then she lay down. Brian had left her enough slack so she could get to the water and drink and once in the brush Brian peeked back, well out of sight, and the dog got up, drank a bit, then lay back down and seemed to go to sleep.

Brian worked carefully, slowly, used his best abilities at watching for sign, studying everything he could, and found almost nothing to help in the mystery of the dog.

He started with a small circle, or half circle since it ran from the lakeshore, out three hundred yards and around and back to the lakeshore and on this first loop he saw the dog's tracks in soft mud in a small clearing coming from the north.

He began to work in that direction, making small arcs, but he found only one more mark, again to the north about a hundred yards from the first one, a dog footprint in soft dirt and just a tiny touch of blood on a leaf.

That was it.

It would have been easier in the fall, and of course much easier in the winter, in snow. In the fall there were no leaves and the grass died back and it was much easier to see things. Now, with thick foliage, you had to be standing almost on top of a track to see it, and he could find no more.

Maybe, probably, the dog had come from the north. That was it. He didn't know from where, how far, or even if that was the true direction. The dog might have come from the east and turned south when it heard or smelled Brian. Or from the west.

And no deer either.

Oh, he saw sign. He found one pile of dung that was still warm to the touch but the brush was too thick to see a deer, let alone get close enough for a shot.

He came on a snowshoe rabbit and decided to take it. He changed to a field-point arrow—he'd been walking with a broadhead ready in the bow—but the arrow caught a twig on the way and deflected slightly so the rabbit was hit low, in the gut, and had time to scream before he got a second arrow in and killed it. They gave a piercing scream sometimes when they died. Brian had heard it many times at night when predators caught them—it was nerve-wrenching and sounded like a baby screaming for its mother. He hated it.

But more to the point, the scream—and this was probably why it had evolved—alerted all animals within a quarter mile that a predator was hunting and that was the end of hunting, for two reasons. One, all the small animals went into hiding and the deer left the area. Two, the scream brought other predators that were curious about the kill. All wolves, coyotes, hawks, cats, weasels, fox, owls, eagles, marten, fisher—any predator—in the immediate area headed for the scream and that ensured that the rest of the small animals *stayed* in hiding. Probably the only exception to this rule were ruffed grouse, which seemed to be so dumb that nothing really affected them, but they had excellent camouflage covering and in this thick foliage it would be next to impossible to see one, though they had good meat, dark meat.

So rabbit it was, and fish, and aside from chastising himself for making a shot when there was a twig in the way, Brian was grateful and thanked the rabbit.

He worked his way back to the campsite, keeping one eye open for a grouse, but he saw none. He found the dog sitting by the end of the canoe, still tied—she had heard the rabbit scream, and Brian coming, and gotten up to greet him.

"Hi, dog," Brian said. "We have food. I'll get some more in a bit and make a stew. . . ."

The dog wagged her tail and stood, moved against the rope and Brian untied her and had to lift the rabbit high to keep the dog away from it.

"Not raw," he said. "Not the meat. I'll give you the guts in a minute. . . ."

He set his bow aside, took out his knife and made a neat incision up the middle of the carcass, scooped the entrails, heart, liver and lungs out and gave them to the dog, which virtually swallowed them whole and then cocked her head, tail wagging gently in the puppy begging stance, asking for more.

"Some manners . . ." Brian smiled and thought of himself when he had first come to the bush. Watching a dog eat raw guts would have brought his stomach up.

But he had seen both wolves and coyotes kill now

and the entrails were their favorite part. And this dog was more wolf than not; a pure, friendly carnivore.

He skinned the rabbit and stretched the skin high in a tree to dry. The hide was thin and fragile and very far from prime and would not wear well, but he had in mind trying to make some lures with the hair and tiny hooks he had brought to see if he could use a willow as a pole and fly-fish some of the streams between the lakes for trout. He had seen them often beneath the canoe, some of them quite large, but they were very spooky and didn't seem to want worms for bait, and wouldn't stand for a shot with an arrow.

He made a fire and put some water on, using his largest aluminum pot, and dumped the rabbit carcass in whole, then covered it with a lid that slid down around the outside about an inch to keep the ashes out.

Then he took one of his fish arrows, without the bow, left the dog on the bank and let the canoe drift out a short distance into the lily pads, held the arrow over the side with the triple-barbed point about a foot underwater and wiggled the point, held it still, wiggled it again.

And here they came. Small bluegills and sunfish, four or five inches long, so curious they couldn't stand not to get close, and with a sharp motion he jabbed the point down and took one in the side, flipped it into the boat, pulled the point out and put the arrow back in the water.

In twenty minutes he had ten fish and he took them to shore, scaled them with the back edge of his knife, split them neatly and fed the guts to the dog again before he dropped the fish, heads and fins and all, into the stew, which was boiling nicely.

From his pack he threw in a handful of rice, "To give it body," he said, smiling, to the dog, and then, "Come here. Here."

And the dog came to him and leaned against his leg with her good side and held her head up to be petted.

"You're a friendly girl, aren't you?" Brian rubbed her ears and studied the wound in the bright day-light. The sewing didn't look half bad but now he could see that there were other lines as well, scratches, as if the dog's side had been hit with a small, very deadly rake.

"Something with claws," Brian said. "Not dogs, not wolves, not teeth. Cat, big cat, panther, or bear."

There it was again. Bear. It almost had to have been a bear and either the dog ran off from its home for some reason and into a bear or . . . what? Was attacked and *then* ran off?

"No." He shook his head, absentmindedly petting the dog. "I wish you could talk—this doesn't make any sense at all."

The pot on the fire boiled over and he used a stick under the wire handle to lift the lid off and check the contents.

The rabbit meat had started to separate from the bones and the fish were right on the edge of disintegrating so he set the pot aside to cool and threw some green leaves on the hot coals. The day was starting to warm up and the black and horse- and deerflies were getting active. The smoke would keep them at bay while the stew cooled and he and the dog ate.

Then what?

He had a friend now, a new friend, and he smiled, thinking, First dog, his first dog, although technically she wasn't really a pet and truly belonged to herself more than she did to Brian.

But she was a friend, a friend in need, and as the cliche said, a friend in need was a friend indeed. The cut seemed to be starting to heal, although he worried about the flies and thought of boiling up some kind of mud to sterilize it and putting it over the cut to keep them off. In a week or so he would cut the stitches out.

But he would need more food now than he did for just himself, and for that reason, he thought, he felt a sense of urgency that he had not felt before.

A need to go, to move.

But there was no real reason for it.

And yet it was there, the odd feeling, the odd push in his mind.

No plan, no direction, just a strange unease as if there was something he needed to see or do or hear or feel somewhere . . . where?

All right. From the sparse sign Brian had found, it seemed that the dog had come from the north.

So he—no, not just he anymore, they—*they* would head north. The Cree summer camp was up there on that arrowhead lake with the island, maybe twenty, thirty miles. He would go see his friends and maybe they would know where the dog came from and even if they didn't he might be able to meet Susan, Kay-gwa-daush, and tell her about the beauty mark.

Now they would eat the stew and he would make a sterile mud pack for the wound and they would head north. Just a nice, leisurely trip to see old friends.

But still he found himself pushing, hurrying, and he didn't really know why.

CHAPTER

7

Brian boiled lake mud and packed it, still wet but not hot, on the wound. Much of it fell off but some stayed and seemed to help and while he was doing it he thought of a better solution. He would get spruce and pine gum from tree sap where it formed on the trunks and melt it and put that over the wound. That stuff stuck to everything. He thought, I'll do that when we stop this evening. He smiled. He was already thinking and saying *we*—it was like the dog had always been there.

He ate a little of the rabbit meat and two of the fish and gave the rest to the dog, still in the pot. And the dog ate everything, fish heads, bones, rabbit bones, meat, and then drank all the broth and looked at Brian in open gratitude, wagging her tail and folding her ears down in a submissive gesture.

"My, my, you were hungry, weren't you?" Brian cleaned the pot and loaded the canoe, wondering how it would all work. He had become competent with a canoe, perhaps even expert, but he had never tried to take a large dog with him. Canoes were not the most stable of craft and a dog going crazy would pretty much upset the whole applecart. He tied the cargo down well and used a bit of cord to lash his bow and quiver so that if they rolled all the gear would stay with the canoe.

He needn't have worried.

He pushed the canoe into the shallows, turned it until it was sideways to the bank and turned to get the dog but she jumped in ahead of the cargo and sat down and waited for Brian to get in.

Clearly, Brian thought, the dog had been in canoes before—as she would have done if she had been a Cree camp dog.

He pushed off and had not gone twenty yards when the dog's full stomach, the warm sun and the rocking motion of the boat combined and the dog lay down on the floor of the canoe and went to sleep.

Brian stroked evenly, using a long reach and a straight pull back to move the canoe in a steady flow forward. There were thousands of lakes in the north country, and almost all of them were connected by streams or small rivers. The general flow was north, or northwest, although there was a lot of meandering through low hills. Brian moved to the north end of the lake looking for the outlet and saw a beaver dam across the stream that flowed there.

He had to unload the canoe on top of the dam, lower it by hand and repack it in the stream below. It was the only thing he didn't like about the Kevlar canoe. It was light and wonderfully strong, but too flexible for hard work. He knew the Crees had heavy old thick fiberglass canoes and when they came to a beaver dam like this they would simply get up a head of steam and just slide over the top of it, down the far side and off into the stream.

But the dog jumped nimbly out of the canoe and back in with no problem and they followed the stream four or five miles, moving through several ponds and over five more beaver dams before coming to another lake.

Because of the time spent going over dams it was coming on to evening, time to find a place to stop before dark so he could catch some fish and maybe do an evening hunt for a small deer.

They had seen four moose during the day, feeding in the ponds, and two of them would have been easy kills. Brian had come very close on one of them, a small bull. But still, he was over six hundred pounds and even with the dog that was too much meat to deal with and he didn't want to waste it.

The dog's reaction to the moose had been interesting. Rather than bark or whine or even make a fuss the dog had merely crouched in the canoe, laid its ears down to lower its silhouette and watched in silence, now and then looking back at Brian as if to say, "Aren't you going to shoot?"

He found a flat place near the outlet to the stream into the next lake and pulled in to shore.

"Out," he said to the dog, which he had been doing with each beaver pond, and the dog obeyed. Brian let the canoe drift back out and used the fish arrow to spear a dozen small panfish—there were hundreds under the lily pads. He used a piece of string for a stringer, which he fed through their gills, and left them in the water to keep.

He tied the dog up again, took the bow with his quiver and moved into the brush. From the canoe he had seen another clearing farther up the shore and he knew white-tailed deer liked to come in to clearings in the late day, probably to get away from the flies in any evening breeze. He moved as silently as possible through the trees and thick willows toward the clearing.

He stopped and watched a rabbit move past him and freeze into what would have been an easy shot and a quick kill. Good meat, but he felt confident about the clearing and didn't want to take a chance. He had become extremely good with the bow, exceptional. Twice now he had taken grouse on the wing, an almost impossible shot. He knew he was good.

He was good with a bow because his eyes were

quick and he saw "inside" things, where the arrow had to go, and "saw" the arrow almost as a line of light to the place where it should hit. Not a target, not for fun. As an extension of his mind, in an almost Zen state, but for one thing and one thing only.

To hunt.

To see where the arrow would have to go to make food, to make meat, to make, oddly, life out of death. The Cree family had thought him strange at first because he still used a bow while they had 30-30 rifles. But then they had seen him shoot and seen how much a part of the kill he became, with the bow and arrows he had made for himself, not with these modern laminates and truly straight shafts, and they had thought him like the Old Ones, the ones who knew the Old Ways, and had respected him for it.

He stopped well short of the clearing, before he could see anything and before any deer could see or hear him.

And this time he was rewarded.

There were four deer in the clearing. Carefully, he inch-step by inch-step moved to the edge of the thick willows and parted the leaves with the point on his arrow, nocked in the bowstring, ready.

Two doe, two bucks, one old with a large rack in thick velvet, the other a young spike buck with small single antlers in even thicker velvet.

The old buck would be too tough and fat. Doe

had the best meat, but he hated to shoot them because there was a slight chance they might be pregnant.

So it was the young buck.

The deer did not know he was there and he waited patiently, controlling his breath, waiting, waiting.

Twenty yards to the young buck, maybe less. Fifteen. A bird flew from the other side of the clearing and the deer were startled by the sudden flight but it was merely birds squabbling and they did not run.

The buck took a step, paused, stood not fifteen yards now from where Brian hid in the willows, then turned its head away.

Perfect.

Brian drew the broadhead back until it nearly touched the bow, sliding the wooden shaft on his finger so it wouldn't make a noise rubbing on the arrow rest on the bow, aimed just above the shoulder blade knowing the arrow would drop a bit in flight, held for an instant to be sure . . .

Then released.

The arrow flew clean, left the willows without touching anything and seemed to disappear against and then into the buck.

The young buck jumped, seemed to arch in the middle, took three faltering steps and lay down on its side.

Brian waited. The other deer still had not run,

were merely watching the small buck as if curious, and Brian stood that way, quietly letting the arrow do its work for a few seconds, and then the buck laid its head over, facing east, as so many animals did when they died, and the light went out of his eyes and he ceased to be a deer and became meat, food.

Thank you, Brian thought, thank you again, and still he stood and still the other deer did not run although the bigger buck came over and smelled the young one as it lay dead.

Then Brian stepped out into the clearing and the whole world blew up. The deer exploded in huge bounds that had them out of the clearing and gone in fractions of a second. Brian moved to the small buck.

He poked it with his bow to make sure it was truly dead. The arrow had gone clean through and lay in the grass on the other side ten or twelve feet away. Brian picked it up and used his fingers to wipe the blood off and squeegee the feathers so they could dry straight.

Then he cut the deer's throat to bleed it and began the drag back to camp. He would normally have dressed the deer out and left the guts but he wanted them for the dog, especially the heart and liver.

It was four hundred yards to camp, not very far, but through thick brush. It was almost dark by the time he had dragged the deer back.

The dog whimpered when he arrived and wagged

her tail and Brian put a pot of water on to boil—he was dying of thirst—and gathered wood for a long fire. He would be dressing and skinning and cutting the deer after dark and would need light.

"Big feed," he said to the dog, taking out his knife and the stone. "Big feed tonight and tomorrow. We'll stay here and eat."

And from the way the dog was wagging, so hard she nearly fell down, she agreed completely.

CHAPTER

8

But in the morning Brian had changed his mind and couldn't explain why. . . .

He had skinned the deer and rolled the hide to stretch later—it would keep for a day or two—and the dog had eaten the heart and liver and lungs in one sitting. Easily five pounds of meat. And then chewed on scraps while Brian cut the rest of the deer into manageable hunks, two back legs and two front, the meat from along the spine—the tenderloin—which was the best meat but on this buck very small.

He had read somewhere that wolves could eat up to twenty pounds of meat in a single meal and he thought the dog was coming close. She . . . just . . . kept . . . eating.

Brian cut pieces of raw meat off and threw them to the dog and even when her stomach was so distended Brian was worried about it stretching her skin and opening the wound, she still ate.

He put a stick by the fire and hung meat to cook and ate the tenderloin, probably three pounds, until it was gone and then roasted a front shoulder and ate some of that, but the dog didn't stop until Brian finally quit handing her meat.

Then she dropped like a stone and was asleep when her head hit the ground, sound asleep, gone. Brian smiled and squatted by the fire and studied the dog sleeping.

He had watched her during the day, learning about her, amazed at how the dog keyed to him and he keyed to the dog. When the dog was sitting up, looking around, Brian found himself watching her, watching for a reaction, depending on her for warning in case something came. It was all new, the bond, and he wondered how he could have lived his whole life and never had this, never had this closeness with another species, with a dog. It had been a great loss. He decided he would never be without a dog again.

In some way, the dog filled a hole in his life, filled a loneliness he hadn't even known existed, and he wondered if it had always been the same for men; if somewhere back in time in a cave a man took a wolf pup and sat him down and thought, There, my life is better now. Well, not that way exactly. But something like it, something ancient man had recognized, some connection, because when he thought about it, it seemed that almost all cultures had dogs with them to work and enjoy or—and he shuddered—to eat. He went to sleep sitting by the fire thinking that the next day they would lie around, eat more of the meat and then dry, or try to dry, into jerky what little there was left.

. . .

Dawn, first light, found him packing the canoe to leave. So much of what drove Brian now was instinct, feelings, what he used to call hunches but what he now thought of as logical flows of information from his subconscious based on knowledge that he sometimes did not quite understand.

Usually, it was right and he had learned to trust it. When he had awakened this morning something, an inner force, had made him pack the canoe and get ready to head out.

North. Where he thought the dog had come from—something pulled him north. And now there was a distinct urgency he still could not understand except that it had something to do with the dog and the wound and the fact that he was sure a bear had done it and there was no reason for the dog to leave its camp simply because a bear had hurt it . . .

Unless.

And he could not think of the *unless* with logic because there was no logic to it. Just the urge to go, to make a start.

And so he packed the canoe and when it was packed he tied cord to the two back quarters of deer to hang them over in the water. The coolness of the lakes and rivers would keep the meat fresh for at least a day. He slid the canoe out sideways to the bank and signaled with his hand for the dog to jump in and by the time the sun was over the tops of the trees and warming his back he was stroking the canoe across the lake.

He had in mind, if there was any true plan at all in his thoughts, to find the Cree camp and ask them if there were other trappers nearby and see if they had had a problem with a bear.

That was as far as his thinking went, along with the fact that it would be nice to meet Kay-gwa-daush. He should have been happy, or at least felt pleasure at going to see old friends, but instead he found himself pulling harder at the paddle all the time.

Clawing ahead, frustrated that pulling the two deer legs through the water slowed the canoe, not smiling, not happy at all, but reaching forward harder and harder with the paddle, ripping the water back alongside the canoe . . .

End of lake. Another beaver dam. Over it, reload, back in water, dog in canoe, tearing down the stream, looking ahead, always ahead and not even thinking now, just pulling the canoe forward.

End of lake. Beaver dam. Stream through swamps, more dams, more work over them, stroking, stroking to yet another lake.

And then dark.

He had not stopped the way he usually did, still in light, to find a place. He took a clearing with a slight angle and stumbled around in the dark to find wood and it was truly late by the time he was ready to get water on to boil and cut pieces of meat to make a stew.

He gathered more wood in the dark, made a hot fire to get the water boiling as fast as possible and did his daily gear check by firelight.

When he finished, the stew had boiled and he drank the broth, ate the meat, fed the dog from the rest of the back leg and lay down to rest.

He ached and was tired from paddling hard. Sleep should have come fast but he lay on the grass, his mind tumbling, wondering how far there was yet to go. He had thought it wasn't over thirty miles, from the way the camp had been described, but he had come close to thirty miles today and didn't seem to be near a big lake, although a lot of that travel had been back and forth because the country was flat and the streams wandered. He knew for a fact that at one point he had paddled two miles east and west to go less than half a mile north.

The dog seemed to be affected by his mood and even after eating did not lie peacefully and sleep as she had the night before but instead sat near Brian, almost leaning against him, looking into the darkness and periodically whining softly and the direction it was looking was north.

Something there, Brian thought, there was something up there the dog knew about and didn't like and he knew it must have been what caused the wound and the way the dog was looking, trying to see through the darkness, her nostrils flaring as she tried to get a smell, her ears perked for any sound, whatever it was must be getting closer.

Brian threw some leaves on the coals to make bug smoke and slept, finally, on the ground with no shelter except for a Polarfleece pullover draped over his side. He was up before dawn, starting the fire again, heating water to drink, feeding the dog a bit of meat and into the canoe and paddling at first light.

At first he was stiff and his back sore, but the lake was about a mile long and by the time he reached the outlet at the end the stiffness was gone and he was back to clawing with the paddle.

More beaver dams, more streams, another lake, then another series of dams and streams and swamps and then a change.

At first he wasn't sure what it was—something was different. It was the same water, the same canoe, and he paddled the same way but there was a change around him and when he was moving along the edge of a stream under an overhang he realized what it was—the woods were different here.

There was less sound, less small movement. Before, there had always been something happening, some indication of nature, and here . . . it had changed.

A quieting that wasn't there before, and not caused by the canoe passing. Before, the canoe had had no effect at all. But he hadn't seen a moose in hours, and before, they had almost been common; he hadn't seen birds, but more, hadn't heard them either.

There was man here; he was getting close to man.

And in another mile the stream he was following widened into a shallow entrance to a large lake that led away to the north. It was at least five miles long and widened rapidly to the left and right as he entered it and then seemed to narrow to a point at the end, five miles away.

The lake was shaped like an arrowhead, or nearly so, and more, even in the afternoon heat mist he thought he could see a large island at the far end.

It was the right lake, where his friends were camped, and he pulled the remaining deer leg back into the canoe to make the paddling easier and started pulling for the island. But it was as if the Fates, having been kind to him for so long, decided to make up for it. A breeze started coming from the north, with clouds, and it quickly turned into a wind, then a strong wind hitting him head on, and where he had been making three and sometimes four miles an hour he was now down to barely one, and some chop was splashing over the bow.

He slid sideways to the left, close to shore, but while the chop diminished and he was no longer shipping water the wind was still as strong and the trip across the lake that he'd thought would take little more than an hour was suddenly a six-hour pull, and that only with hard work.

Still, his stomach was full of good meat and water and he was strong. He kept up the pace, accepting the three-quarters of a mile an hour as it came to him, and after four hours was only a mile and a half from the island when a new strangeness hit him.

The wind had been blowing straight from the island to him, all his way across the lake, and yet he smelled nothing. If they were camped there, on the island, they should be burning fires for cooking and heating. But he could smell nothing.

Not the slightest whiff of woodsmoke. The wind was blowing directly at him from the island, right across him, and there was no odor.

And the dog . . .

She was up now, on all fours, whimpering more loudly than ever before, mixing those sounds with low growls, her ears up, then down, then back up again, listening, then hiding, then listening again. Aggressive, but worried?

Brian paused and something made him reach out

and take a broadhead out of the quiver and lay it across the bow even though the moment without paddling cost him his forward motion. He thought, This is silly, I'm being a worrywart, but positioned the bow close to himself just the same.

Then dug with the paddle again, pulling hard for the island, the dog whimpering and growling.

I just wish, Brian thought, I could smell their smoke.

CHAPTER

9

At first he thought they were just gone, perhaps back to a town for some reason, although he knew they hated cities as much as he did.

But no dogs barked to greet him, and there was no noise at the island, no sound, not even birds singing. By the time he pulled the canoe up onshore next to one of their canoes—a thick glass–hulled eighteen-footer—he knew something was wrong.

As he pulled in the dog jumped from the canoe onto land but did not leave him, did not run up the shore. She stood near him, pressing against his leg while he tied the canoe to a limb.

He took his bow and put his quiver over his back and nocked a broadhead in the string and thought, All right, crazy as this is, I'll just take the teasing if they see me walk up all ready.

From the beach where their canoe had been tied a track curved up about fifty yards to a camp area and he could see they had constructed a cabin about fifteen feet square with unpeeled logs and a tarp for a roof pulled over a ridgepole to make it peak and drain off water.

But no people.

All right, they were gone. That was too bad but they would come back and . . .

The door to the cabin was open. It was made of three rough planks chopped from soft pine and hung on leather hinges—he could see that much when he was twenty yards from the cabin—but it stood open and they would not have left the door open that way.

The dog stopped, her nostrils flared, and all the hair on her back went up in a thick ridge and she growled in a low, steady rumble.

Brian put his three pulling fingers on the bowstring, ready to draw and release, and moved closer to the cabin.

Then the smell hit him. Not smoke, not woodsmoke, but the smell of blood, musty, rotten smell of spoiled blood and flesh. He stopped again, flaring his nostrils, taking the offensive odor in, trying to see all around and up and down at the same time, holding his mouth open and his breath to hear better and that was when he heard the sound of flies.

All right, he thought. All right. They left some

meat here and something broke into the cabin and got at it and let the flies in and . . . and . . . and . . .

It was all wrong. So wrong. He had never felt anything so powerfully wrong in his life and everything in him wanted to run, get away from this place, but he knew he had to go on, to go in the cabin. . . .

He stood to the side of the door, eight feet away. "Anybody in there?" Then, to the woods, more loudly, "Is there anybody here?"

Nothing. Just the continued buzzing of flies, no other sound, and he stood another second and a half, nervously fingering the bowstring; then he took a deep breath, held it and stepped into the cabin.

There were no windows—the only light came through the doorway and from a dim glow that worked down through the tarp roof—and for moments he stood inside the doorway virtually blind in the sudden darkness.

Then he stood aside and let the light in and at the same time his eyes became accustomed to the darkness.

"My god . . ."

The words slipped out without his knowing, or caring. It looked like a bomb had gone off inside the cabin.

Sacks, boxes, sleeping bags, bunks, snares, traps and provisions were torn open, thrown everywhere, ripped opened and flung in piles like so much garbage.

But no people. So they had gone somewhere, maybe in the plane, and probably a bear had gotten into the cabin—and indeed, he saw slash marks on a sack of flour that could have come from bear claws—and torn into everything. . . .

But no, that was too easy. There was more and part of him knew it, knew there had to be more, though he didn't want to admit it and he saw then what he had missed at first.

The flies. There was a buzzing of flies everywhere but the sound was deceptive because the flies were all back in a corner where torn sleeping bags covered something, something . . .

Brian moved to the corner and with no breath left now, only fear, he reached for a corner of the torn sleeping bag and pulled it away and saw the body, a human body doubled up and jammed back in the corner, covered, and it was Kay-gwa-daush's father, David, destroyed, face torn, neck torn open, one arm ripped half off the body, stomach torn open . . .

"Arrggh!" Brian turned and instantly vomited, almost hitting the dog, which had followed him into the cabin, growling openly but crying and whining as well, looking at the dead man. "Oh my, oh my, ohmy-ohmy . . ."

He couldn't think, couldn't react, couldn't *do* anything except stand and throw up and try to make what he had seen not exist. It couldn't be. It just couldn't actually *be,* not this, not this terrible thing. . . .

But he turned back and David was still there, in a cloud of flies, and a part of Brian's brain went on automatic and saw things he could not stand to look at, could not bring himself to openly acknowledge.

David was dead in the corner. It couldn't be but it was, he was there and torn terribly apart. It had to have been a bear. A bear, a rogue bear, had broken into the cabin suddenly and attacked and overpowered David and killed him. . . .

He had fought, or tried to fight. There was a rifle, a 30-30 in the corner by the body with the lever pulled open. David had tried to load it and the bear had come so fast he hadn't had time to get a shot off. Perhaps the gun had been in the corner and the bear had burst in and David had tried for it and the bear had gotten him first. . . .

What of the others? There was David's wife, Anne, and the little boy and girl. And Susan. Kay-gwa-daush. Oh god, he thought, oh god, what of them? Where were they?

He turned away from David—there would be time later for what was necessary there—and looked through the rest of the trash in the cabin, turning over paper and bags and bunks. There were no other bodies.

Outside then; David later, but outside for now. There had to be sign. He had missed things coming in because he'd been nervous. There must be sign, tracks, and when he went outside he was appalled at how much he'd missed on the way up to the door of the cabin.

There, in the soft earth to the side away from the hard-packed trail down to the lake, were clear prints of a bear, a large bear, a huge bear. The prints had to be nearly six inches across and even taking into account the way they spread in soft earth the bear had to be over five hundred pounds.

The tracks coming toward the cabin were far apart and dug in hard, as if the bear had been running, running to break in? That didn't make sense. And then he saw boot prints as well, running toward the cabin on the same line as the bear, and it made more sense.

David had been outside when the bear attacked and he had tried to run to the cabin and get his rifle. Had nearly made it. Had gotten his hands on the rifle and worked the lever but the bear was chasing him, was right on him and after he killed him had torn the cabin apart.

But Anne, and Kay-gwa-daush? Had they been outside as well?

The prints leaving the cabin were more measured, closer together, and he started after them and then stopped, thinking of the rifle, and then shook his head. He was not familiar with firearms and might miss if he ran into the bear, and besides, a broadhead was an incredible weapon when it got inside an animal.

He turned away, the bow ready, walking slowly, stopping every few feet and listening, listening. Whatever had happened, he thought, had happened days before; the condition of David's body and the movement of maggots in the wounds told that.

"Anne? Susan?" He called several times but knew better. If they hadn't answered when he first yelled coming to the camp they weren't going to answer now. There had been two younger children as well, a small boy and girl, but he could not remember their names. Surely they weren't dead as well. . . .

The kennel. There had been three or four dogs there, not loose but tied with short chains so they wouldn't rip the gear up, and the bear's tracks went at first back to the kennel and three dogs lay dead there, mauled only slightly. A fourth chain was there with a ripped nylon collar on the end and he looked back at the dog, which was still following him. "That was you? And you ran? But why not stay if Anne and Susan were here. Or the kids?"

Unless, he thought, unless they were dead. Please no, just please no, not any more, not now. . . .

But to the left of the kennel there were bear tracks heading off into the brush and alongside the tracks there was a skid mark as if the bear had been dragging something heavy.

No. Please no . . .

It was not hard to follow the tracks and they didn't

go very far. Forty yards back in the brush he found the second body, partially eaten, the buttocks and thighs gone, lying on its face, the head hidden by black hair, the rest of the body covered with leaves and dirt as if buried to save for later.

Please no . . .

He was sick but this time did not throw up and instead squatted by the head of the body and moved the hair away and saw that it was Susan's mother, Anne. Her face was not torn but there was a strange angle to her head as though she had been struck very hard and it had broken her neck.

He fell back, weakened suddenly, and sat in the grass next to the body. Then he stood and left the body as it was—time for what had to be done later, when he'd found out about Susan and the other children—and moved back to the cabin area.

Trying not to think about the bodies—and this was nearly impossible—he forced his mind into a hunting-tracking mode and looked for sign. The water between the island and the main shore was very shallow, never over a couple of feet, and he quickly found where the bear had waded across and come onto the island's shore. Huge tracks in wet mud, then muddy tracks in the grass, moving through low hazel brush up toward the dogs and the kennel, where the bear must have smelled the dog food, fish and beaver meat—the odor would carry with good wind for miles.

Everything in him wanted to hurry, to run, to scream her name and run, but Brian forced himself to be slow, to be careful.

The bear's tracks were even, just walking, never hurrying until the last moment when he cleared the hazel and the dogs saw him and probably started barking.

There, by the kennel, he saw the tracks of two people, one large and one slightly smaller, David and Anne, and there was a dented bucket. They were probably feeding the dogs. The distance from the line of hazel brush to where they were standing wasn't ten yards, thirty feet, three bounds for the bear and he was on them.

Two seconds' warning, at the most, and he was there, on top of them, dogs screaming, one blow for Anne, and Brian could see where her body hit, then David running for the only hope he had, the rifle in the cabin, the bear's prints wheeling and digging as he went after David and the rest in the cabin. . . .

Then bear tracks back to the kennel, where he must have killed the dogs. All but one, the one with Brian, and then more tracks, bear tracks, around where Anne's body had fallen and then the skid marks where the bear had dragged Anne away into the brush to feed.

No other new tracks. No small children's tracks by

the kennel or from kennel to house. No tracks of Susan. No newer tracks at all.

Maybe she was gone, gone to town, visiting friends or relatives back in the world, gone with the children.

He started a circle search, around the center of activity, the attack site and cabin, looping through the brush, close in at first, moving out four feet with each loop, looking intently, studying carefully each stick, each blade of grass, and on the tenth loop he found it and then felt stupid for not having seen it at once.

On the trail up from the lake, just to the side, two scuff marks as if somebody walking, somebody smaller than Brian, smaller than David, had suddenly stopped and then run, frantically run back down to the bank, and there were more skid marks where a canoe had been shoved away from the bank and here, hidden in the tall grass at odd angles, lay two canoe paddles where they must have fallen from the canoe when she flipped it over and pushed it into the lake.

She'd had no paddles, must have used her hands.

And there, at the side, more bear tracks where the bear had run down to the shore and then moved sideways, along the bank, probably following the canoe for a short distance.

On the ground by the first scuff mark was a small two-quart bucket and scattered around it were raspberries.

Susan. No smaller tracks, no children's tracks.

She'd been off in the canoe along the shore picking raspberries and hadn't been there at the time of the attack. Two canoes. He shook his head and winced at his own ignorance. Of course they had two canoes. All the gear and people couldn't travel in one.

Susan had taken the other canoe and gone berry picking either on shore or the other end of the island. Had come back later, after the bear had fed or before, but after the attack and the bear had surprised her, no, seen her coming and gone to meet her and then chased her back to the canoe and out into the water. There were bear tracks in the soft mud of the bank off to the south side that he had missed before when he'd first arrived and they went for a considerable distance, out of sight.

So.

The bear had attacked, maybe fed on Anne but had still been around, perhaps rummaging further in the cabin when Susan returned from berry picking.

Perhaps she called, sensing something was wrong, and the bear had heard her and gone after her. But she was close to the canoes and had gotten back in and out in the water, into apparently deep enough water, before the bear could get to her.

Fast. She'd been fast. The bear had cut the corner and not run the trail—which explained why Brian hadn't seen his tracks coming up when he first arrived—and she still beat him. God, he thought, she must have been terrified; worse, far worse, she had no idea about her parents.

But why hadn't she come back? It had been two, three days judging by the fly eggs and worms, and she still wasn't there.

And where were the smaller ones? Brian hadn't seen any of their tracks nor, he swallowed uneasily, any other signs that they'd been nearby when the bear attacked.

Had the bear gotten Susan and the children, taken them somewhere else?

"Come on," he said to the dog. "Stay with me. . . ."

He moved at a trot down the shoreline of the island, the dog now slightly in the lead, heading south, and the bear tracks lined out in front of him along the bank, through the willows and hazel brush, but always close to the shoreline. Now and then the tracks lunged at the water, then back. . . .

God, he was playing with Susan. She was working the canoe along the shore, trying to get away from the bear and get back to camp from the other side, and the bear was *playing* with her, teasing her, jumping toward her whenever she came too close to shore.

All around the island, and then off, as she must have hand-paddled toward the main shore and when Brian waded across the shallow water he saw where the bear had followed her down the main shoreline as well. But then, after a hundred yards or so, the bear had tired of the game and stopped and moved back in the direction of the island but up into the trees and harder ground and tight grass and Brian lost his trail there.

All right, *then* why didn't she come back to the island? Or a better question was why did the bear stop following her along the shore?

Brian came up with two reasons. First, she had moved away from shore, out into the lake, and with only her hands to paddle she could not move the canoe well. If a wind came up, even a small wind, it would blow her where it wanted and if she was lucky it would blow her out into the lake, away from the bear. If she had been unlucky and the wind blew the canoe into shore . . .

He shook the thought off. The second reason she might have stayed away from the island was that it became dark. Paddling by hand, splashing and clawing, trying to move possibly against the wind and making all the noise in the world, there was no way she could bring herself to approach the island in the dark with the bear possibly, probably, waiting for her. No way.

So she worked her way into the deep part of the lake, or more probably the wind took her, the prevailing north wind, and blew her all night to the south end of the lake, into the large marsh and willows and swamps Brian had come through.

He might have passed not too far from her on his

way north. Or she might have blown to shore on the east side.

And there she might be. Without a paddle she could never get the canoe back north and it would be suicide to try to work by foot along the bank with no weapon.

He stopped, looking at the shoreline and the dog. Her whimpering had stopped and her hair was down. The bear was nowhere near.

He would have to go back, get his canoe, find Susan. She had to be somewhere south on the lake, trying to work north, trying to get back.

He started jogging back, the dog keeping close to his side. Evening was coming and part of him knew that he should bury Anne and David but he knew it would have to wait.

They had to find Susan.

Find out what happened to the children.

Before the bear.

. . .

They found her just before dark.

He and the dog had been walking the shoreline, scanning the edge of the water and peering out toward the center of the lake as they kept a wary eye on the edge of the woods.

She was four miles down the lake, on the east shore, dragging the canoe along the shallows on the lake edge so she could jump in and push out if she saw the bear.

He saw Susan long before she saw him because he was watching the dog and saw when she lifted her nose, catching the scent of something, someone, familiar and loved. Susan was intent on watching the thick foliage on the shoreline. When she was just a hundred yards away he called.

"Susan!"

And it startled her so that she jumped into her canoe as if to hide and when he got closer he saw that she was half crazed with fear and exhaustion. And he understood. He had felt the fear himself and she probably hadn't slept in two or three days and nights.

"It's me, Brian. . . . You don't know me but I spent some time with your family. . . ."

He pulled up alongside her canoe and held the two together.

"Bear . . . ," she said. Her hair was matted and there were scratches on her face and arms. She had been in the water so long she couldn't speak without her teeth chattering. "Bear . . ."

"I know. I know. Here, wrap in this and go to sleep. I'll pull you back." Brian took his sleeping bag and reached across into her canoe and wrapped her in it and forced her to lie in the bottom while he tied a line to her bow, fed it back and started paddling, pulling her canoe behind him. The dog jumped into the first canoe, settling near Susan, who didn't notice her presence through the crushing exhaustion that overtook her as soon as she sat down.

It was into dark by this time and there was a stout evening north wind and a chop. It would take five or six hours to pull the two canoes against the wind back to the island. Good. She needed the rest. She did not know about her parents yet, or had only guessed, and when she found out it would be terrible for her.

Any rest she could get now would be a godsend.

CHAPTER

10

The world came to them.

Not at first. At first there was a time Brian did not like to think about or remember but knew he would have in his mind for the rest of his life.

She had been virtually unconscious when they arrived, back at the island, just at dawn. He had left her sleeping and the dog leading—always in front now—her hair down, no sign of the bear, Brian had taken the time to wrap the bodies in blankets and ponchos and pull Anne back to the cabin and use a shovel to make a shallow grave in a clear spot by the east wall and bury them next to each other.

Then he had tried to clean the cabin a bit and had buried the dead dogs in another shallow grave and then gone back down to the canoe and washed in the lake repeatedly before waking her up and holding her and telling her that her parents were both dead.

She had guessed that something terrible had happened because they had not come looking for her but even so the shock was profound. She had sobbed for hours while he sat there, on the bank of the lake, his bow next to him and the dog sitting a little away, holding her while she cried, feeling as helpless and awkward as he had when the badly wounded dog showed up. Between sobs, he was relieved to learn that the other two children, Paul and Laura, were visiting relatives in Winnipeg.

Then she had gone to the new graves and put crosses made from boards on each and then gone into the cabin. Brian had tried to straighten some of it, and used lake water to wash where her father had lain. In part of the wreckage that he had not uncovered, she found a shortwave radio with a transmitter. It had been knocked sideways but she put it back on a shelf and hooked it to a storage battery and the radio still worked. She called the authorities and Brian was amazed at how fast things happened. Not three hours after she called, a plane landed on the lake and three men got out, the pilot and a Canadian Mountie and a Natural Resources ranger. They talked to Brian separately from Susan and asked him details he was glad she didn't hear and when it was done they stood by the cabin.

"You have relatives to stay with?" the Mountie asked Susan. She nodded. "An aunt and uncle in Winnipeg . . ."

"We'll fly you there," he said. "If you want we'll gather your stuff for you."

"No. I'll get it." She moved to the cabin and the Mountie turned to Brian.

"I've heard of you. You're that boy who survived after the plane crash."

Brian nodded.

"Do you want to fly out?"

Brian shook his head. "I'll stay."

The Mountie studied him for a moment, then nodded. "As you wish." He turned to the Natural Resources ranger. "And you, are you going to kill this bear?"

The ranger shook his head. "There are many bears here, perhaps scores, within ten or fifteen miles. We wouldn't know which one to kill."

Brian stared at him, started to say that they had tracks, they knew the bear by his sign, they could find him, but he held his tongue. It wasn't the same for everybody, the bush. They had planes and guns and radios and GPS but in some ways they had no knowledge *because* they had all the gadgets; they missed the small things because they saw too big.

Brian had never seen the animal but knew the bear

intimately, how it moved, how it turned, how it thought. They could be looking right at it and all they would see would be weight and girth and hair color and genetic codes and biospeak and would never really know the bear.

He said nothing. But he understood that they were wrong. He knew the bear. He would find the bear.

Susan came out of the cabin with a canvas bag full of her things and they hugged and she saw what he was thinking, what he had to do, because she whispered in his ear, "You must be careful. He is not like other bears. He is a devil *muckwa,* a devil bear. Be careful. . . ."

Brian at first said nothing, still holding her, then said what was most in his mind: "I need to see you again, when this is done. There are things that need to be said."

She nodded. "I understand. I left a letter for you, in the cabin. My address and phone numbers are there. I'll wait. Find me when you come out. . . ."

Then Susan and the men climbed onto the floats of the plane and into it and the pilot spun around and took off and in moments Brian was alone with the dog, even the sound gone.

Just the lake and the island and the woods . . . and the bear.

The bear was still out there and it was not right,

not now. The bear had been wrong, had gone too far.

Brian would find him.

And he would kill him.

It was personal.

THE HUNT

He left the canoe but he took the dog, his knife, the bow and his quiver, light moccasins, a plain dark T-shirt and a lightweight, dark green pullover.

He took matches and one small aluminum pan. He did not know how long this would take, only that he would not stop until it was done, but he wanted to travel as light as possible.

When he waded the shallows and went to the main shoreline he stopped and used dark mud to streak his face and neck, then slid into the foliage following the bear's tracks. He would lose them later, he knew—they were very old tracks anyway—but in the meantime they would help him to further understand and know the bear and he would hold them as long as he could.

Initially the bear moved along the shore, working in the soft mud, following the canoe with Susan until the wind blew it away from him; then he turned and went up, away from the lake.

Here the tracks were muddled in the soft pine needles and harder to follow, although the dog seemed to have been paying attention to Brian and moved ahead with her nose down. At first Brian was dubious—he still did not know dogs that well—but again and again when he lost the tracks and followed the dog he would come upon the tracks once more and after an hour of on-again off-again tracking he began to trust the dog completely.

It was like having another sense, not to mention a kind of early-warning radar. The smell was old and the bear long gone, Brian could tell that by the relaxed attitude of the tracking dog. They moved well together, and Brian learned more about the bear.

He was lazy. He did not climb hills but worked around the base of them instead, turning logs, ripping stumps, and he had distinctive paw marks. One claw was gone on his left front paw and one broken in half on his right. In mud or soft dirt it was easy to read him, know him, and just before dark Brian came on a place where he had lain to rest or sleep.

In some deep grass the bear had matted down an area to make a bed. Brian felt the ground, not sure what he was looking for, a touch, a feel of the bear, but there was nothing. The grass was cool, and had dew forming on it and the dog was still not nervous so Brian moved off to the side and made a small fire and heated water and chewed on a piece of jerky he'd found in the cabin.

Then he drank, put the fire out, moved back into the brush and settled in to rest. He did not think of sleeping, not yet, but halfway through the night even the mosquitoes weren't enough to stop him and he trusted in the dog's warning ability and dozed enough for his mind and body to rest.

Before light he was moving again, still following the dog when he couldn't cut open sign, but by mid-day he decided that following the meandering track of the bear would not be fruitful. He figured he was perhaps four or five miles from the lake where the attack had happened and the bear was clearly not moving in any pattern, was just wandering, looking for food.

He would stay in the area and Brian could accomplish more by getting to what high ground the terrain afforded and hunting downward, trying to get ahead of him, knowing the bear hated to climb hills, and he left the scent trail and climbed a nearby low ridge.

For a moment the dog hesitated, standing on the scent trail, whining softly; then she seemed to shrug and follow Brian up the ridge, dropping into position just in front of him, ears perked forward, nostrils flared to take in the most scent.

And they worked that way most of the day, hanging to the tops of ridges, moving slowly. Brian would take a few steps, stop, listen, watch the dog's back hair and ears—how had he lived so long without a dog, he wondered again and again—and they saw bear.

Three times he saw bear, one small female, two even smaller yearling cubs, but they all moved away from him and the dog when they saw him and when he moved to where they had left tracks he knew they weren't the bear involved in the attack.

He knew the attacking bear's tracks, how his right front paw toed in slightly, along with the missing claw and broken other claw, like a signature.

And no new sign all that day. Not until evening.

They had moved across a ridge that led up a small hill and somehow, hunting along the ridges, he had come back to a hill he'd moved across before.

He did not know it at first, not until he crossed the top, the dog moving just ahead of him, and he saw a place where they had stopped to listen and rest. He recognized a scrub oak tree he had leaned against because it had a twisted, bent fork about four feet off the ground.

"Well," he whispered, his voice sounding strange to him, "we've come around. . . ." He stopped because the dog had changed. She had been smelling the ground and her back hair suddenly stood on end and she growled.

"What . . ." Brian moved to where the dog stood, looked at the ground, but it was thick with humus and grass. He could read nothing. He held his breath, as the dog did, and they listened together but he heard nothing and he looked back to the ground and did not see anything until he had gone three yards farther along his own old track and there, where the grass had been worn by a white-tailed deer scraping, there was soft dirt and smack in the middle of the dirt there was a perfect print.

Large, huge, missing claw, perfect sign and very, very fresh.

It was the bear.

The Bear.

And it was following him, tracking him.

Hunting him.

Hunting *him*.

And for just that second, that long, long second, Brian went from predator to prey, felt a coldness on his neck, felt as a deer must feel when the wolves pick up its scent, as a rabbit must feel when the fox starts its run . . . cold, no breath, everything stopped. No thinking. Just that long second of something even more than fear, something very old, very primitive.

The bear was hunting *him*.

Then it was gone. The coldness, the fear were gone and replaced by something even more pure, more primitive, as he thought of what was coming, what the bear's tracks actually meant.

He did not have to hunt the bear any longer. It was hunting him, it would come to him, and it would be soon, soon.

Dusk now, he thought, dark in an hour, if it takes an hour. I passed here, what, three hours ago, and if he's moving on my trail, how fast? Faster than me, certainly, he could be close, very close. In that split second he happened to be looking at the dog, saw the dog's head turn to the left, and he dropped and turned at the same instant, heard brush crashing as he fell, brought the bow up, tried to pull the broadhead but too late, all too late.

The bear was on him, rolling him, cuffing him. The bow was knocked out of his hands, flying ahead, arrows spewing out of his quiver, the bear strangely silent, pushing, pounding him as he first rolled in a ball and knew that wouldn't work, not now, not with this bear. This bear had come to kill him and he was *going* to kill him and there wasn't a thing Brian could do about it. He tried for his knife but the bear knocked it out of his hands, knocked his arms sideways, grabbed his left arm in his jaws and flung Brian back and forth the way he would worry a small animal.

I'm not going to make this, Brian had time to think. He's going to win again, he's going to kill me, and then he heard the ripping growl of the dog and it landed on the bear's back and grabbed and the bear turned to hit the dog, knocked it sideways twenty feet where it lay, stunned, and then the bear turned back to Brian.

But there had been that second, two seconds, and Brian was lying on the ground well away from his bow but the arrows that had flown out of his quiver were all around him and he grabbed a broadhead with his right hand—his left hung useless—and dove, following the arrow, into the center of the chest of the bear.

He was amazed at how easily it slid in and he saw only six inches of arrow showing and thought, There, that's it then. . . .

But it wasn't. The bear snapped at his chest, at the arrow, broke it off, and Brian tried to get away in that instant but the bear wasn't done and grabbed him by a leg, pulled him back, and as he slid over the ground he came across another arrow and he grabbed it and turned and jammed it up into the middle of the bear and it *still* wasn't enough and the bear cuffed him, slammed him alongside the head, and he went down and the last thing he saw was an enormous wall of fur coming over him and he thought, All right, this is how it ends.

This is how it all ends.

And everything tunneled down to nothing but a

point of light and then that went dark and there was nothing left.

. . .

Sounds, soft whimpering sounds. For a second, he thought, That's me. Everything was still dark, he was being crushed under some great darkness and then he smelled the bear, on him, around him.

And heard the sound again. It was the dog, licking his face, pulling at his shirt. The bear was on top of him, lying still, dead where it had fallen. The second arrow had, finally, brought death.

Brian pushed, pulled at the ground and the bear and finally got free. It was dark, though not pitch-black, and in the early light, limping and holding his left arm in, he found wood and got a fire going.

With the light he looked first to the dog. The original stitches had held, unbelievably. But she had a new wound about four inches long across the top of her head. There didn't seem to be any other obvious injuries and with the dog settled Brian turned to himself.

Bites in the arm, on his leg, but not great tearing wounds. His left shoulder seemed to be dislocated and as he tried to raise his arm he heard a *pop* and it snapped back into place with a burst of pain that put him on his knees and brought splashes of color to his vision.

"Oh man . . ."

But no other serious damage. He didn't quite believe it. Not at first. The bear had seemed to be all over him, hitting and biting, and he'd thought the wounds would be much more serious. . . .

He turned to the bear. The dog had walked around the carcass, her hair still up, growling with bared teeth, but when the bear hadn't moved, and was obviously dead, she had moved closer, peed on the bear's leg, back-kicked dirt onto the body and walked away to sit off to the side licking her left rear leg where she had a small cut.

The bear lay dead and Brian tried to find some feeling of triumph, as the dog had, some sense of victory, but all he could think of were David and Anne and the great loss that Susan and her brother and sister had in their lives now. He had thought there would be more. He even hoped that he would feel more. But there was nothing but the loss of his friends.

And a dead bear.

Not a villain, not an evil thing. Just a dead bear. Like any other dead animal that he might have hunted. Killing the bear did not bring back his friends, did not ease the pain for Susan and her brother and sister.

It was just what it was, a dead bear.

And he would have to clean it now, skin it, pull the carcass down to the lake and get his canoe and take it back to camp and use what he could, not waste any more than he had to because in the end it was as wrong to waste the bear as it was to let it live after what it had done.

In the firelight he found his bow and arrows and knife and small aluminum pot. The pot was dented but he pulled the edges apart and made it serviceable. It was not far to the lake and he brought water up and boiled it and gave some to the dog and drank some himself. Then he boiled mud and put it on his cuts and the dog's head to keep morning flies away and then took the knife and turned to the bear.

There was much work to do.

AFTERWORD

I can almost hear the voices: "You said the last Brian book was the *last* Brian book," and I did say that. But the response from readers is still profoundly over-whelming, hundreds of letters a day, all wanting more of Brian, and so this book, and I will no longer say that I will write no more about Brian and the north woods. . . . In some way he has become real to many, many people and they want to see more of him and so, and so . . . we shall see.

As to the subject of this story, it is hard to imagine any animal as evil—only man would seem to have a capacity for true evil and deliberate cruelty. And bear, especially, lend themselves to seeming likable. They have been romanticized to a point far beyond reality. What bears truly are has been lost in concepts like the teddy bear and Winnie the Pooh and I can well understand how some people will view the bear and the attacks in this story. Some years ago, just after the movie *Free Willy*—a film about a captive killer whale that a boy helps to freedom—had come out, I was interviewed on a radio call-in show and mentioned that I had seen two killer whales playing with a baby seal, throwing it back and forth like a toy before killing it and eating it, and the phone almost jumped off the hook. Killer whales are friendly, people said, which is sometimes true, and they only eat fish, which is not true—they not only eat seals but often dolphins as well, and off the coast of New Zealand a female and her calf attacked a scuba diver. They are wolves of the sea, if you will, and for a killer whale to eat, as with wolves, something else has to die.

And so to bear: the truth about bear is that they are cute and smart and, sometimes, lovable, and they also kill things and have on more occasions than some people like to admit attacked and killed and eaten human beings.

I have had bear come into my sled-dog kennel and kill dogs to get at their food—one particular dog, Hulk, was killed with a single blow in the middle of the night. My wife has been chased from the garden to the house by a bear, which almost caught her. It had a small terrier named Quincy hanging on its neck fur all the way. And I have a friend whose nephew was in a scout camp in Wisconsin and a bear pulled him out of his tent at night and tried to carry him off and eat him and only let go when dozens of scouts attacked the bear with rocks and sticks and forced it to drop the boy, who had to get hundreds of stitches and has not fully recovered the use of his arm.

And the attack in this story, a couple killed and the woman partially eaten, happened almost exactly as I describe it; the bear attacked them on an island in a lake in the Canadian woods where they had come in a canoe to fish, killed both of them and dragged the woman off to feed.

We don't like to think of ourselves as prey—it *is* a lessening thought—but the truth is that in our arrogance and so-called knowledge we forget that we are not unique. We are part of nature as much as other animals, and some animals—sharks, fever-bearing mosquitoes, wolves and bear, to name but a few—perceive us as a food source, a meat supply, and simply did not get the memo about how humans are superior.

It can be shocking, humbling, painful, very edifying and sometimes downright fatal to run into such an animal.

GARY PAULSEN is the distinguished author of many critically acclaimed books for young people, including three Newbery Honor books: *The Winter Room, Hatchet* and *Dogsong*. His novel *The Haymeadow* received the Western Writers of America Golden Spur Award. Among his newest Random House books are *The Glass Café; How Angel Peterson Got His Name; Caught by the Sea; Guts: The True Stories Behind* Hatchet *and the Brian Books; The Beet Fields; Alida's Song* (a companion to *The Cookcamp*); *Soldier's Heart; The Transall Saga; My Life in Dog Years; Sarny: A Life Remembered* (a companion to *Nightjohn*); *Brian's Return, Brian's Winter* and *Brian's Hunt* (companions to *Hatchet*); *Father Water, Mother Woods* and five books about Francis Tucket's adventures in the Old West. Gary Paulsen has also published fiction and nonfiction for adults, as well as picture books illustrated by his wife, the painter Ruth Wright Paulsen. Their most recent book is *Canoe Days*. The Paulsens live in New Mexico and on the Pacific Ocean.